Christmas in July

LIBBY SCORES

Christmas in July

Book Cover by Elizabeth Scozzari

First edition 2025

ISBN 979-8-9987816-4-3

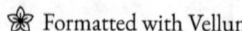 Formatted with Vellum

Content Warning

For those of us (still) waiting for Santa to come and stuff our stockings—ho, ho, ho!

Also, a _MASSIVE_ shout out to my proofreader who fields a lot more than short deadlines and Santa Smut. Don't waste too much time wondering if I too have my nipples pierced!!!

June

"Y ou're going to Greece tomorrow?"

I'm pacing around my apartment jumping out of my skin waiting for Emma to tell me *everything.*

"We are!"

"Wellll?"

I squeal. I can't help it. My best friend is going to one of the most beautiful places on Earth with one of the most gorgeous men I've ever seen. If you're into the tall and perfectly polished type.

"Are you okay?"

"Am I okay?" I repeat back. "I'm about to pee myself and it's not even my trip."

"You also don't have to meet anyone's entire family." My heart skips a beat and for a second I forget how to breathe. "Sab, in your nose girl. You're *not* meeting the family.

"Right."

"Shit."

"Yet," she says.

"Bitch."

"One day you'll have to meet them."

"You're so in love."

I roll my eyes, and then look down at my area rug. There is a clear indication of where I've been pacing back and forth.

"Guilty," she says.

Her happiness is radiating through the phone. I love it! I love her! And Errol and all of it.

"Enjoy it!" I try to remember the good things about my last trip, and not the fact that I was stood up. "You deserve it!"

"So do you," Emma said. "And you'll find it. So stop moping."

"I'm not *moping*," I say. "I'm celebrating your love."

"You are, while you're *moping*."

"Least I'm not *annoying*."

We're both laughing too hard to finish egging each other on.

"Girl," she says. "Since you've been back from England the only thing you've climbed are some mountains. And I don't want to know how many books you've read."

"So I'm taking myself off market for a bit––"

"We are beyond off market. You are in some kind of slump. And it's not working for you."

I walk out of the living room and into my kitchen. All of the ingredients for a red wine hot chocolate are on the counter. Having a relaxing night in with a book hotter than ghost peppers isn't moping, it's self-care or some social media bullshit term.

"I'm content, Emma."

"Which is for lame, normal people, Sab. Of which you are neither." The ice in whatever she was drinking rattled. "I'm not even sure you're a person sometimes."

"It's a fair question."

I start to measure out double of everything. It's an early start and a big book.

"It's a month. Too long for me to be worrying about you isolating. Promise me, you'll do something fun with yourself."

"Everything is fully charged--"

"Not what I meant."

"I know."

"I'll call you before we get on the plane tomorrow. I love you."

"You too, Em."

I'm looking at the bottle of cabernet sauvignon in front of me. Usually I am all in for white wines, especially those with a twist off, but red seemed sexy and fitting. And I wasn't sure if white really went with hot chocolate.

"Here goes nothing," I say to myself.

CHAPTER 2

Kris

Why is she putting wine in her hot cocoa? And why is it red?

"What're you doing?"

I groan at my brother's voice. I swipe my hand over the giant crystal globe and turn to face him.

"Not involving you."

"Because you're still stalking that girl?"

"The only *stalker* here is you, Kyle."

He walks closer to me, peaking over my shoulder.

"She's really that good of a fuck?"

I shoulder check him and start walking out the door. He's the one that taught me how to use the stupid thing for more jolly and less wholesome reasons.

"Whatever," I say.

My voice is barely above a growl.

"Seriously, Kris," Kyle says. "What's up with you?"

"We're not having some heart to heart so you can tell me *this is why I only look.*"

"We're not," he says. He throws his arm around me and directs me over to the wall of portraits. Every Santa in our family hangs there looking down at us. "Because unlike me, you're not betrothed or likely to end up on the wall for a very long time. Why not pursue your love interest?"

I turn toward him with my eyebrows raised.

"What do you need?"

"Nothing man," he says. He takes his arm back and turns toward me. "You're grumpy as fuck lately. I thought we busted each other's balls because I'm the older, better looking brother, but you're just mean."

I sigh, playing back the past few months. He's not entirely wrong, not since I had to cancel on Sabby's trip to England––the one that I set up for her and where she fucked a leprechaun, not that she seemed to know that––I have been a bit out of sorts.

"Probably not the best vibe for a future Santa."

"Maybe just a future Satan."

I roll my eyes.

"So you're gonna help me get the girl?"

"Depends on how bad you fucked it up."

"Why do you assume it was me?" I snap back. My tone is sharper than my words. "Withdrawn."

"Exactly my point." My brother jumps, putting me in a head-lock. "Mom's making supper. While you and I set the table we're going to make a game plan."

My fingers tremble and my book slips from my hands.

"Yes."

I moan to an empty apartment. My stomach drops and I arch my back.

"I am a good girl."

My nails dig into my breast as I cry out. The MMC won't hear, but I don't care. If my panty vibe had ears it would be so proud of me.

I ride out my orgasm taking a minute to compose myself, ... the toy out & I pick my book back up. There's something ... comforting about the vibrations. I get a flash of Emma's ... face and clear it from my mind focusing instead of the ... 6'4" tattooed and the head of a motorcycle club bad boy with a heart black diamonds. He's primal, dark, and gritty. Only for the FMC does he shine. Of course he just pierced her nipples as punishment for getting herself off without his permission, so there's that.

I shudder, shifting my hips to hit that one spot—ohhhhh I shiver letting the goodness course through me. I find my book ... in the blanket, tucked between me and the couch. My can't focus on the words. My body is still tingling. The buzzy hot cocoa has made an impact.

Instead, I throw a napkin into my book and find the remote for the toy. The buzzing stops and I'm aware of how quiet it is. I sit up and finish what's left of my now-lukewarm-cocoa. It's late, way later than I meant it to get. I shrug, it's not like I have anything to do tomorrow.

Emma's on her way to meet her future in-laws and I have a hot date with a trail and the rest of this book.

I hear her voice in the back of my head, before she can kill my afterglow I say, "hiking isn't moping." Not that she can hear me. Maybe I shouldn't be spending so much time alone. Talking to characters in books and my bestie like she's here, when she's very much not.

If there was ever a character in a book to talk to though. I conjure my mental picture of this baddie biker and throw a glance to the purple remote. It's not the worst way to fall asleep.

I clean up the living room and make my way to the bedroom. I strip down to everything but the toy. My reflection in the mirror catches my eye. I wonder how I would look with pierced nippies. I doubt the piercer would be an alphahole dom, but a girl could dream. I pull up the browser on my phone. There's a tattoo/piercing place close by. I click on the calendar. They're booking three weeks out.

"Good for them!"

Leaving my phone on the nightstand, I hold down the power button and a soft buzzing sound fills my ears. I slip between my covers and let the sensations overtake me as I drift off to a euphoric sleep.

CHAPTER 4

Kris

"This is a dumb idea," I say.

"It was yours!"

My eyes shoot over to my brother. He's not wrong, but I had been thinking ahead, not in the moment.

"We were spitballing!"

"You were stalling." He rolls his eyes at me. "Like now, we're already here. Check her calendar, pack a bag––"

"We're not kidnapping her."

"Not yet, but you wanted to do a Christmas in July thing. It'll be much harder if you don't have clothes for her."

"How many women have you kidnapped?"

My brother looks appalled at the suggestion.

"None, but Elise watches all those Hallmark movies. Those guys are always prepared. Which you, bro, are clearly not."

I'm torn between wanting to sucker punch Kyle, and be impressed. Instead I make my way toward Sabby's bedroom. Walking past her kitchen, it looks like she finished the bottle of red. Between that and the small pinch of Christmas magic we borrowed for this, she should keep asleep.

Stepping into her room I'm met with the sounds of her breathing, heavy and steady, in the background it sounds like

13

there's a bee somewhere. My eyes follow her legs, bare sticking out from her blanket. A thin sheet covers her tits, her nipples pebbled and perky underneath. My cock jumps in my pants at the thought of biting down on them.

"Focus," I tell myself.

I trace the rest of her body, the swoop of her collarbones, the curve of her neck, her jawline that looks fucking edible, those lips. I'm straining against my jeans, and by the time I get to her eyes my dick and my heart are heavy. I start to lean forward, wanting to kiss her lids, but the sharpness of my zipper brings me back to reality.

Shaking my head I look at her nightstand. There's a remote looking thing next to her phone. I pick up both. The smaller device is smooth and texturally pleasing, some kind of silicone maybe? There's a power button and a larger one. I nestle in my palm and open her phone.

It's unlocked.

I fight the urge to wake her up and ask what the fuck? I take it as a blessing and go to her calendar. There's a few reminders for pre-orders and when library books are due back. She doesn't have a work schedule, but I could have sworn I've seen her working this summer.

Her emails provide some insight. The office she works at is closing for the month of July. Emma will be in Greece with *Errol?* I make a note to see if it's the god of love, or just some poor, unfortunate soul. The names people come up with these days are wild. She's going to be alone for the summer.

I go to close the apps and see an internet page: Black Sun Piercing. My thumb taps on it. They're busy since the next appointment Sabby could make was for the middle of July.

"Interesting," I say.

I close the apps I opened and return her phone to the table. I press the big button on the remote and the vibrating sound gets louder. The pattern has shifted.

Sabby moans and rolls in her sleep.

She didn't, I think.

I lift the corner of the blanket up. She draws her leg under and lifts her hips.

"Well I'll be."

I grip myself through the rough fabric, wincing at the teeth of the zipper. I press the button a few more times, jerking myself up and down each time. Her breathing shifts, I watch as her hands claw at the sheets.

This is her setting. The sheet shifts exposing her nipples. They look delectable. She's moving with the vibrations, my hand following her lead. She moans. It could be my ears but it sounds something like *Kris.* Her body trembles. I work the tip of my cock out in time to cum into a shirt I found on the floor.

Looks like she'll be getting a new one of these for Christmas, I shrug, balling the shirt up. I return the controller and make my way to the living room.

My brother is sitting reading a book.

I blink, but he's still there.

"Dude," I say.

He jumps, nearly throwing the book.

"Your girl is a freak," he says.

He points to the book. I can't see the title but across the cover is a motorcycle and Lily of the Incas.

"We can talk about it on the way home," I say.

Kyle looks up at me, a smile emerging.

"Not the only freak I guess," he says.

He points to the shirt and the top of my pants, which I forgot to fasten.

"She's sleeping."

"Kris."

His voice is stern. I'm taken aback since Kyle is the most laid back out of all of us. I groan, annoyed at myself for the situation.

"No dumbass"

"So you just jerked off watching her sleep?"

I refuse to answer that. Instead I gesture to the door.

"Are you coming or what?"

My brother laughs as he stands. Before I can hear whatever comment he's about to make I open the front door and step out into dad's workshop. He'd be disappointed we used it, but our mom would be livid. I'm relieved when Kyle steps out behind me. The quicker we're in and out the better.

Nothing to see here, I think. I toss the shirt in the fireplace and watch as the flames eat away at it. On the table there's a box with Sabby's name on it. Easiest replacement present ever.

"Not my kink," Kyle says. He's sitting down on the brown microfiber sofa. "But it might be your girls. That book she was reading? The guy ties her up, some biker dude, Gray I think, and pierces her nips as some sexual punishment thing."

Disappointment stabs me in the chest. It wasn't *Kris* she was moaning, it was *Gray*. That's certainly a punishable offense.

I feel myself stiffen in my pants, and hope my brother doesn't notice.

"It's wild man," he keeps talking. "The shit these women are reading. And writing! Dad said the uptick in books last year was a lot. I don't think he really stopped to see what kinds of books were being asked for."

"Probably better," I mutter.

"So what's the plan now that you've done some reconnaissance."

My plan is to go to my room and fist fuck myself into oblivion.

"Not sure yet, but I have some ideas."

July

I wake up aware that I am not in my bed. Not in my apartment or in my bed back at home.

"Fuck."

My body aches how I imagine running the Self-Transcen-... feels like. But I wasn't running... 100 miles around the same... Queens — I've never actually been to the borough. The... weeks have been the same combination of work in morn-ing and reading in the afternoon, and then more reading... chocolatey treat at night.

The only variation is when Emma FaceTimes me.

Emma. Maybe she'll notice that I'm missing. She's been in Greece a week now, but that can't be enough time to forget about your bestie, right? Friday was my last day at the office, they won't be open again until August, so there's no way they'll know I'm missing.

... wakes my body up. Maybe J. D. Salinger was... ...a victim of abduction. I look around the...

looks like a hunting lodge. A place you'd expect bikers or serial killers to hide out in. I'm not saying she was right twice, but maybe once I get home I find a book that's not a dark romance.

"Stay calm, Sabby."

I roll my eyes at myself. I'm not chained up, so that's a good start. The shirt I'm wearing isn't mine. It looks like it, but the hole just under the left boob isn't there. Not that my B cups took advantage of it, it was still nice to have.

My feet touch the ground, I'm not wearing pants, panties, or a bra, but thick wool socks cover my feet. *Weird*. I straighten out and look around the room. A laugh fills the space, loud, jolly and somehow menacing.

"Fuck!"

It's full-bodied and there's something about it that makes my thighs rub together. *Really* not *the time*. It reminds me of my mall Santa. He couldn't make it to a vacation *he planned*. I'm sure he's not responsible for kidnapping me.

Dread pools in my stomach. It would be preferable to have that giant slice of beefcake stroll in here than whatever psycho I'm now sure has taken me.

"Zabaglione." My breath catches. I'm not sure if I'm turned on or angry. Possibly both. "Have you been a good girl?"

"Not gonna work twice."

I ignore how wet I already am, and focus on that fact that this holly-jolly mother fucker kidnapped me.

"Then why are your thighs glistening?"

"Working up a sweat on my getaway," I say.

I'm walking toward the door when I'm paralyzed. It was a flash, a quick zap around the neck.

My hands reach up to the collar there. I hadn't taken notice of it before. Did he put a shock collar on me? I feel my nipples tighten. *No, Sabby. Stay focused!*

I close my thighs. It feels delicious. *On getting away dumb ass.* I scrub at my face with my hands.

"Let's go."

I straighten out my back and start walking toward the door again, ignoring the second jolt as best I can. My pussy tightens, and I shiver, but I'm not giving him that satisfaction. I'll give that to myself later.

"You're really being a bad girl, Zabaglione"

Chills spread down my body. This is absolutely not okay. The way he says my name makes me feel like an untamed cat. I want to run my nails down his front until he's dripping blood. Would only be fitting for how he ripped my heart to shreds, or for him taking me. *Asshole!*

"Because being a good girl gets me anywhere with you."

I put my hand on the doorknob, surprised by the double jolt. I push down and am surprised that it opens. It didn't occur to me that it could be locked until it swung free.

"Do you want to be punished?"

It sounds like he's smiling. Part of me would love to see what he comes up with. The last time we had sex he spanked me like I stole something and I had been on my best behavior then. I'm annoying myself. I groan and take one step outside of the door.

My face smacks into something clear. I can't see it but I sure as shit felt it. I blink a few times. My vision must be a tad blurry because it's the most transparent plexiglass I've ever seen.

"You're not running off, my little sugar plum."

"Do you have some sort of Christmas fetish?"

I whip around shouting at the empty room. Engaging in verbal warfare isn't the same as giving in.

"Oh baby girl, you have no idea."

I roll my eyes.

"Well, I won't be choking on your candy cane, so have a great day."

I walk toward the back door. There has to be some way out of here.

"It's bigger than a candy candy." I hear him muse. "But I'll make sure you choke on my eggnog."

There is no reason that should turn me on. But the thought

of swallowing this man's load makes me throb. He's not in the room, if he is I haven't seen him yet. I check out the room in my periphery. Minimal decor, lots of wood, no Naughty Santa looming in the corner.

My hand catches on the knob. This door is locked.

"Ass clown mother––"

"You have a filthy mouth." He growls. "It's going to look so good wrapped around me."

The sound of heavy footsteps fills the space. My body tingles in anticipation.

His hand wraps around my throat and pulls me against his body. He's just as turned on as I am, I can feel him pressing against me through that soft, velvety fabric he had on last time I saw him.

"Do you not own––"

My question is smothered in my throat. I can feel the pressure going to my head, clouding my thoughts. Edging me on to fall apart in his arms. His other hand trails up my thigh. I lean back against him.

It catches the hem of my shirt and keeps moving up, sending shivers everywhere. He passes alongside my nipple, my moan catches in my throat where his other hand is still fastened. He stops right next to my lips. I resist the urge to lick myself off of him.

He spins me around, I take one breath in before his hand is back around my throat. I'm dripping down myself, onto his knee now tucked up against my slit.

His eyes are dark with a bright sparkle. He squeezes tighter and I open my mouth. I watch as he licks his finger. I feel his spit land on my tongue. It's warm, but I can't swallow. The pressure is making me lightheaded. I start to sag. His body is the only thing holding me up.

"Do you remember the safe word?"

Fuck, fuck, FUCK!

He laughs. His body moves against mine, the sensation

against my clit drives me wild. He loosens his grip on my neck and leans into my ear. His words dance against my skin.

"It's red," he says. "Triple tap if you can't speak."

It's the first time I've heard warmth in his voice. I might come just like this.

"Do you even remember my name?"

Bastard.

He releases me, I swallow his spit, tasting both of us together. I look up at him. A few months ago I would have gotten on my tippy toes to kiss him. Now I know him better. There's a clanking of metal and I look down to see him cuffing my hands. As annoying as it is, he seems to know exactly what I like.

Kris turns me back around and scoops me up. I try to kick myself free, but my legs flail uselessly in the air. He plops me back down on the bed. Metal clashes against metal and my other wrist is cuffed.

"You've really been bad, Sabby."

"Not as bad as I can be."

I don't get the satisfaction of telling him off again before there's a gag ball against my lips.

He looks down at me, his eyes are piercing but I refuse to fall for it this time. Sex god or not, he ghosted me. I raise my eyebrows, so much for him stuffing my mouth.

"Don't worry, sugar plum." He runs his fingers up my throat. "That will come later. But first."

There's a tear as he rips my shirt open. His fingertips scrap against my breasts forcing my back to arch.

He fills his hands with them, kneading them like dough. I didn't know they could bend so far back. It hurts but it feels so good I'm panting. He eases off, going for the nipple tweak instead. He pinches down, twisting until I cry out. It feels like pin pricks from the corners of his nails.

My body writhes underneath his. He flicks his tongue down my jaw, along the side of my neck. It's still sensitive from him choking me. I moan. He keeps working his way until he catches my nipple between his teeth.

I grunt, salvia drips out the corners of my mouth. If I wasn't gagged I would have cried out his name. The look he's giving me silences me.

"What was that?"

He speaks with my left nipple still in between his teeth, the right one is pinched between his nails.

"KEYS."

"Are you saying 'these?'"

I shake my head.

"What about 'gris?'"

"NO, NO."

"You wouldn't be saying 'gray?' Not again, right?"

My body shifts from play scared to actually frightened. I don't know a Gray, but a few weeks ago I was reading––

"OWWW"

I buck against him, but I'm trapped under his weight.

"This was the toy you had in." He holds up my Leaf, the purple triangle looking silly in his thick fingers. "Reading dirty books with the toys I buy for you."

My thoughts are racing. *Did that toy come from him? Do I tap out and hope he lets me go?*

"I can see you when you're sleeping."

I start kicking and thrashing. He's a madman. There's no way he would know I used that toy while reading my last book. I don't update Goodreads with that much detail.

He grabs my legs and tucks them under his thighs. He's still wearing those ridiculous Christmas boxers, but I can feel the tip of his cock pressing against my center as he sinks on top of me. His lips brush against my ear as he says, "I spied on you once, planning this." That warmth is back in his voice. I feel myself melting underneath him and I'm furious at how wet I am, how much he turns me on, and that he's not at least nine inches deep inside me yet. "If you tell me to stop I will."

His face pulls back and hovers over mine. I raise my eyebrows and shake my head.

"Three taps with the leg then."

I watch his eyes roll and wonder if I can knee him in the balls like this. He sits back up and replaces the head of his penis with the toy. The soft vibrations roll through my body.

I'm going to drown this man in my come.

The friendliness in his face is gone, and the terror in my heart starts again. He nibbles and massages my tits, paying attention to every part of them. I'm headed toward sensation overload with the toy stimulating my clit as he's mauling me. I feel him rock hard resting against my entrance. It's enough to drive me over the edge.

I push against him teasing myself, riding every bit of pleasure I can. He said he's going to punish me and I want it. He reaches for something, the head of his cock nudging my hole.

Something warm and slick slides between us. I open my eyes and look into his. They're almost fully black. They twinkle mischievousness. He laughs like he knows what's coming, and I feel myself release again. I'm so fucked, and I love it.

CHAPTER 6
Kris

The lube catches her attention, but she still has no idea what's in store for her. I'm keeping an ear out for anything that sounds like RED, and also my name––fictional or not, I hate that fucking Gray guy. She's tried to break free and kick me, but hasn't tapped out yet.

I'm wondering if she will.

She's coming off her orgasm, her pussy is still throbbing. The head of my cock can feel it as it rubs small circles around her other entrance. It's not going to prepare her as much as my fingers, but I'll need my hands for her punishment.

I also borrowed a little bit of elf magic for this. It was the part of the plan I didn't share with my brother. He probably thinks we're on a romantic holiday the kind his betrothed, Elise, would enjoy.

The thought starts to kill my mood. One look at Sabby splayed, and I'm right back on track. Her body is gorgeous, but her essence puts it to shame. Even if she's still mad at me, I can sense it, she's into this.

I'm still massaging her tits. They fit snugly in the palm of my hand. It takes a lot of control to not just rip them off of her,

27

they're perfect. But I can't lose control, a little pressure, a little pain. I want her relaxed, drifting between orgasms.

She looks peaceful. Her eyes snap open as I press the button for the vibrator. We're still two settings away from the one that makes her moan. I want her begging for it.

I keep rubbing against her, each time she pushes back on me. My sugar plum is a dark one. She's so juicy, squirting all over me. My shaft glistens where she's come. If I look too long I'll bust all over her ass, which is not the plan.

I press the button. Her eyes open and she's glaring at me.

"We don't like that one, do we baby girl?"

She whines and the sound goes right to my cock. It twitches against her ass and she wiggles against it.

She's so ready. I shift my body, making sure I'm lined up properly. Then I press the button again, she screams and as the head of my cock breaches her asshole. The noise she makes sounds like a wild animal. She tries to slide down on me but I have her hands chained for several reasons. She takes me in so good.

Once I'm fully in I take the needle I've been saving and slide it through her nipple. She howls and comes so hard the toy pops out. I grip her thigh with my right hand, and pump my fingers in and out of her. My thumb swirls her clit. Her ass is so tight I have to move slowly or I'll be done before I finish her punishment.

I look down at her. She's stopped biting the silicone ball. Her jaw is slack, spit trickles down the side. Her eyes are hooded with pleasure and pain. The noises she makes are other worldly. She's driving me insane. As she starts to come down I begin moving deeper and pulling back out until just the tip is in. She squirms and tries to take it all.

"Such a good girl for me." I work my fingers at a slower pace, to match my hips. "You take me so well, like I was made for every inch of you."

I drive in all the way to the hilt. Her eyes roll back into her head and she lifts herself as much as she can.

"That's it's Sugar Plum, take my cock."

She growls and I feel it through my shaft.

"You want more?"

Her eyes open wide and she's looking up at me like a feral doe. I take my fingers out and she scowls. I laugh forcing myself deeper. The toy is still going, still on the setting she likes. As I push it against her, she bucks wildly. I grip her thigh again with my right hand and wrap my left one around her throat.

Her cries vibrate against my palm. I thrust my hips, harder and deeper, keeping the same pace that's driving her to madness. I can see it all over her face, the way her stomach tightens, she is so close. I give her breath and take it away again, not wanting her to come too soon. Right as I see her on the precipice, my balls tighten and release, filling her with my come. I give her one last squeeze and remove my hand.

Sabby's orgasm starts and I take the other needle piercing her second nipple. She makes a guttural sound and writhes against me. I stay in her until her body sags. I pull my cock out slowly, a trail of come oozes out of her.

She shivers and looks up at me. Even with the gag still in her mouth, she's smiling. I stay between her legs and unhook it.

"Damn," she says. Her voice is hoarse. "I'm still fucking mad at you, but damn."

K ris removes my shackles and lays down next to me. I lift my head for him to settle in underneath me and realize there are two very long needles through each of my nipples.

"Um."

It's not the most dignified moment, but it fits the vibe. His laughter does not. Unlike when he has something up his sleeve this one is filled with a lightness that is as annoying as it is endearing.

"Well," he says.

"this should be great."

He takes a deep breath. "Don't actually know where to

He rubs my shoulder as he speaks. It's soft and gentle, and I need him to stop. I shrug my shoulder but he keeps at it.

"Stop that and then start with why there are needles in my tits."

"Stop rubbing your shoulder?"

"Yes!"

"Why?"

I huff and twist to look up at him. He's already baffled once by my love in mincing my words.

"It's something attached people do, and other than when your penis is in me, we're not attached."

Kris opens his mouth to say something, from the look on his face it seems serious. I cut him off.

"Nipples and needles. Go."

This time he sighs and then starts explaining.

"You had an appointment to get them pierced, if you want we'll just swap it out for the bar. I have the standard gauge for new piercings so--"

"How did you know that? And actually, what made you think you should be the one to do it?"

I'm trying not to shout, but this man likes to push me to all of my limits it seems.

"I saw the appointment on your phone, and the book with Gray."

I go to stand up but his arms wrap around my neck and my leg. Fuck his height and wingspan, or whatever it's called for people.

"Stalker! You can't talk to me, but you can stalk me." I'm squirming aware that one wrong move and one of us is getting poked by a needle or I'm losing a nipple. "Let go of me!"

"Zabaglione, please."

The raw emotion in his voice brings the gravel factor to a new level. As if I wasn't already a gooey mess from the bikini line down.

"What, Kris?"

"I'm sorry." Not what I was expecting. "I fucked up. In a whole bunch of ways actually. I shouldn't have slept with you or developed feelings for you. I shouldn't have given you a trip and then bailed without an explanation."

He's talking so quickly and I want to stop him, but there's a strain in his voice. I'm afraid if I do, he won't ever start again.

"I can't give you an explanation, because you'd think I'm certifiable. Not to mention it breaks pretty much everything my family has ever taught me. But I want to, because I've never met anyone like you. The way you think and all of our talks and your heart. I mean your essence it's just--I think about you and the world feels like a better place." He looks down at me. There's a blush across his cheeks and I'm not sure if it's from the lack of oxygen or because of what he's saying. "I'm rambling. I'll shut up now."

I twist my body closer to his, but pull back enough to see his face.

"Just tell me."

"Can I show you?"

I twist my head. Either he's going to go full psycho killer on me or--I can't think of anything else.

"Are you going to kill me?"

"Sabby!" My arms wave around me. I can't actually form words, but it doesn't seem like a stretch from where I'm sitting. His eyes trail down my body. I ignore how his cock stirs and how I quake at the thought. "Fair enough. I'm not going to kill you."

"Okay then."

"But I am afraid you'll hate me."

"I can't hate you more than when you bailed on me."

"Ouch."

I shrug and settle back into his chest.

"You hurt me," I say. "And not in the way I like." He leans forward and kisses the top of my head. *I hate this man.*

"Do you want me to change those out? I did an entire training course online and I practiced on my brother."

"You have a brother?"

"I have 14."

"What!" He shakes his head and looks down at me. "That's 13 more than me."

"Isn't Bastian your half brother?"

"Depends," I say.

"On what?"

"Do you want half a nutsack?"

33

"Noted. I'm sure he's a better brother than all of mine combined."

"I'd agree."

"You haven't even met any of them."

"Don't have to." He squeezes me in a side hug and laughs. For a minute I forgot how mad I was. "So you're going to switch these out and then show me your family secret before bringing me home?"

"Kind of," he says. I lean back and look at him. "I'm off for the next two weeks."

"Even if it's just sex only," I say.

He smirks

"We'll see what happens."

Before I can answer he stands up. I'm staring at his butt, frustrated by how biteable it looks. He comes back with a washcloth. The warmth spreading between my legs. Kris pats me dry and goes back to the bathroom. I think about what he said as the water runs.

He apologized and then said a lot of things that a few months ago would have had me swooning off the bed. Not that I'm not touched, but it doesn't make sense. Part of me hopes that his show and tell will help. If it doesn't I'm not sure I can have sex with him for two weeks and not end up a broken human being.

It took me too long to forget how massive his cock was, that vein that was made for me to run my tongue along, his smile and those eyes. The kindness that radiates from him in the moments after sex, plus each phone conversation.

Ugh, he had drilled through my icy shield, and now that I've repaired it, he's back again.

"Okay," he says, walking out of the bathroom, "hands are washed, gloves are clean, everything is new and sterilized."

I bite my lip trying not to laugh, but Kris is standing at the foot of the bed with his fuzzy boxers back in place, surgical gloves, and a tray of supplies.

"Should I call you doctor?"

"I liked it when you called me Santa Daddy."

I roll my eyes and chuckle.

"I'll bet."

I hadn't meant to say it, but the last time we had sex he coaxed it out of me. Now, I have metal rods he's touching about to give me the rings I was going to get anyway.

"Do you want me to turn the vibrator back on?" My eyebrows raise up in response. "The whole pleasure pain thing."

"I think I'll be okay."

If he was a professional I might take him up on it, but I'm afraid I'll squirm in delight and whoop––there goes my nipple. *No thanks.*

"Get comfy and close your eyes when you're ready."

"I'm good, real––"

"Eyes closed, Zabaglione."

Damn him. My pulse quickens, friction zips between my legs as I settle into place.

There's a tickle along my chest before he lifts my breast. I can feel the needle as he does. It doesn't hurt, but it's surprising even though I know it's there. I feel a sharp nip and then he lets go of my boob.

"Can I look?"

He laughs. The sound rocks through my core. Part of me wants to test him, see what his next punishment will be if he pierced me for saying another man's name in my sleep. I feel an airy touch on my other breast and think better of it.

"You took it so well," he says. The hair on my arm stands up. "You can look now."

I open my eyes and look down at my chest. Other than some redness they look good. Better than I could have imagined.

"You did great."

He shakes his head.

"You sat very still. Better than Kyle."

"Your brother has a name."

"We all do," he says. "All of them starting with a K." I stop

35

looking at my nipples, *they look amazing*, and tilt my chin at him. "Family tradition. And my mom likes the alliteration."

"If you tell me your last name is Kringle I'm getting off this bed right now and––"

"And what? You couldn't even make it out the front door before."

"You're telling me it's Kringle?"

"I'm asking you to do what you said."

I close my lids and take a deep breath in. My whole body sways. I need water and to figure out if this man fucked my body beyond repair.

"Take a sip."

I open my eyes and see a glass of water with ice cubes and a straw in front of my face. *You have a small dick,* I think to myself watching his face for any indication he can read my thoughts.

He doesn't flinch.

"Thank you," I say. Definitely needed water. "Show me."

"First you're going to need to put this on."

He hands me a sports bra, the kind with the clip and the zipper. It's my size, and it's nicer than anything I've owned. I don't wear a bra as often as my grandmother would like.

"It'll keep your new nips safe."

I sigh and take the bra wrapping it around myself, getting the girls settled.

"Anything else?"

"Shirt and pants might be good," he says. "Just in case."

There's something in the way he says it that makes me think of Tim Curry in the 1985 movie, Clue.

"Are you sure you can't hear my thoughts?"

"What?"

He looks surprised.

"I was thirsty and you handed me water. You impersonated Tim Curry."

"Sabby." There's a tone to his voice that I can feel in my pussy.

"I just fucked you feral and pierced you. Hydration should be a given. The Tim Curry thing."

His voice fades out and he walks away from the bed turning around with a look that makes me almost drop my glass.

"You made one fatal mistake." He is channeling his inner Wadsworth like the part was made for him. "One night, on the phone, you told me the colors in the opening credits were some of your favorites. And clouds, though blue and gray in shade, are not often anyone's favorite color."

I laugh until water splashes over the edge, spilling onto my hand.

"Okay, okay."

I say. I drink my water, licking the droplets from my hand.

"That's a good girl."

I get a chill and scooch to the end of the bed. The slight jiggle is enough to make me happy about wearing the bra. It's not as painful as I thought it would be, but I'm extra aware of my nipples. He has clothes laid out for me. My head swivels between the outfit and him.

He's making moves to put on a similar outfit. A grown ass man, with chiseled abs, and butt worthy of being bitten, and a face that begs to be ridden is putting on matching gingerbread pajamas.

"I guess you're serious."

"If I'm only getting one shot at this might as well make it count."

"I swear if you're killing me––"

"I'm not."

"––you better fuck me like that again before you do."

"Dark humor looks good on you, Sabby." I finish pulling the pajama shorts up and look at him. "Just like the pjs."

He comes over and buttons the top for me. His eyes linger on my breasts.

"You can't touch them yet."

I didn't know this was happening, but I did do my research.

"I know that," he says. "We'll see how long I last."

I roll my eyes and shake my head. He sets my pajamas straight and takes my hand.

It's hard to get a read on him, but focusing on that is better than trying to figure out what the hell is going on. It's clear that if he has gone completely mental there's no way I'll physically over-power him. Over our three month telephonic relationship he sounded smart. Not just book smart but *life* smart too.

It was sexy, and now I'm wondering if it might also be my downfall. Not that I'm resigning myself to death by Santa-imper-sonating stranger. I take a deep breath, my breasts moving snuggly with the sports bra, *that's a new sensation.*

I've been so lost in my own thoughts I didn't realize that we're almost back at the front door.

"Eyes closed, Zabaglione."

I roll them again instead.

"So I can't figure out how to leave."

"No," he turns toward me, his eyes almost electric. "Because I want you to be surprised."

I sigh. Even if he doesn't kill me, this man might be the death of me. I close my eyes and we start walking again.

I hear the door open, but this time we don't get stopped by some high-grade plexiglass. There's a chill in the air, followed by the smell of sugar cookies and the warmth of a fire. Joy so real I believe it dances through my heart.

"Open."

I do, blinking several times to make sure I'm seeing this correctly. We're in another room. It's bright and big. It looks like the inside of a snow globe. The wood is incredibly old, but solid. It frames the space and is what both the desk, big enough for a small giant, and matching chair are made of. There's a couch and a fireplace.

"Where, what?"

"This is my dad's office."

"You took me to your parents' place to defile me?"

He laughs. It's louder, stronger here, like someone stuffed it with more happiness.

"No," he says. "I took you to my cabin."

"I don't understand."

"You will." He squeezes my hand. "I hope."

He leads me to the couch, walking over I see two pillows on the floor in front of the fireplace. I tuck in there. He sits next to me. It should be a crime for anyone to look that sexy in cute pajamas.

"The only thing missing is--"

"Hot cocoa." I look away from the fire to him. "What's your favorite flavor?" There's a pleading in his eyes, like this is somehow the most important question he's ever asked me. "Don't tell me, just close your eyes and think about it."

It's not a hard question. I open my eyes, shocked to see Kris holding a mug the size of my head. I can already smell the mint wafting over. I use both hands to take the mug and through a mouthful of whipped cream taste the best mint hot cocoa I've ever had.

"This is still hot," I say.

"It's fresh." He sniffs the air. "Your favorite hot cocoa is mint?"

"That or vanilla, or plain. Depends on the brand, how I'm feeling. Is yours mint too?"

He offers me his mug. I learn forward slurping from it, afraid to spill my own.

"Gingerbread!"

He nods.

"I didn't even know they made that."

"You can switch yours if you want to."

He gestures to the coffee table behind us where a new mug is sitting. Steam rolling off the top, less whipped cream than before. More with how I like it compared to Kris, whose dollop would put Daisy to shame.

"Where'd that one come from?"

"It's all part of what I'm trying to tell you, Sabby."

I take a sip of my own hot cocoa, the warm, liquid chocolate fighting back the nerves of uncertainty.

Before he can say anything the doors open letting in a flood of laughter. I turn and look over my shoulder, there's a man that has to be one of Kris' brothers, an older woman, and an older man, who I assume are his parents. They're all in variations of Christmas or wintery pajamas as well.

I go to stand up, but the coffee table now has three additional mugs of hot cocoa on it and a plate of cookies. Before I can get up the woman calls out, "oh no dear, you stay right there. We can do the pleasantries after. Enjoy your cocoa."

I've walked into the Sawyer family takes Christmas. I look between Kris, and the one I assume is his brother, trying to figure out which would Leatherface.

"Zabaglione," Kris says, "this is my brother, Kyle. And my mom, Jessica, and my dad, Kris."

"Hello," I say. I want to wave but the cup is too big, so I nod instead. *Jessica and Kris... Kringle?* "It's nice to meet you."

"You go by Sabby, right?"

His brother is sitting behind my left shoulder. I twist to make sure I can see all of them.

"I do."

"That's one of Papa's favorite desserts."

I look at Kris' dad and smile. He looks happy but he hasn't said anything yet. For a moment I wonder if he has teeth or if they're just rows of bugs like the Boogeyman from The Nightmare Before Christmas.

"Mine too," Kris says.

I hear Kyle stifle a laugh. I nudge his leg with my elbow. Which makes him laugh harder. Before I can spill it Kris takes my hot cocoa and puts it on the table next to his. The three of us are laughing like silly school children. That's when I notice that their dad is smiling. A perfect row of pearly whites gleaming from his cherry lips.

"If you fit in with Kyle," his mom says, "I don't have to worry about the rest of my sons driving you nuts." I look up at her. In one hand she has her own mug and in the other is her husband's hand. I see her squeeze it as she continues. "These two are my biggest handfuls."

"But I'm your favorite," Kyle says.

"Favorite problem. I'm just her favorite," Kris clarifies.

"You're both wrong." His voice has the soft boom of rolling thunder as he speaks. "I'm her favorite."

"You're everyone's favorite," Kyle chirps.

"Dear, it's different, they're my children. You're my hubby."

I want to throw up at how cute they all are.

"Here," Kris says to me. He somehow holds the massive mug with one hand, his other is on my knee. In a voice so low, it sounds like I'm hearing it inside my head, he adds, "You're my favorite."

I blush, and take my beverage saying thanks.

Kyle clears his throat. Kris looks up at him, all of his family is looking at him. He nods once. I'm either going to be slaughtered or it's time to hear his big truth. This time the thought doesn't make me nauseous.

CHAPTER 8

Kris

U p until this moment I thought having my brother and
parents here was going to be stupid, but now, I'm grateful
they're here.

I'm not really sure how someone tells a person they just
met––months in the span of years is a flash––that not only am I
probably deeply in love with you already, but also I'm Santa
Claus' son, and in line to take over.

Sabby gasps.

His father chuckles.

Kyle is snickering.

His mother makes that weird humming noise when she reads
a romance novel.

"Did I say that out loud?"

"Sure did, Brother."

"Which part?"

My eyes are locked on Sabby who hasn't moved yet. I can feel
the sweat starting under my hairline. *Fuck*.

"That you love her," he says, gesturing at Sabby, "and that
Dad is Santa."

I nod, because what else should I do at this moment? My
heart is starting to race like reindeer at training camp.

"You did say you were in line to take over, but." He leans forward, putting his hand on Sabby's shoulder. "He's very far back in line."

"You boys know that's not true," Dad's voice fills the room. "There's all sorts of--"

"Other times to talk about this, dear." Mom is always the voice of reason and I'm so grateful she's here because Sabby still hasn't spoken. "Let's tackle one thing at a time."

I see her pick up a small plate from the table. There are five all together. Two are definitely the Italian dessert, one is a bowl of ice cream--vanilla if it's for Kyle, but he's not sure what his mom or Sabby are having.

"Sabby," his mom's voice is like a hug personified, when she wants it to be. Otherwise it's like that screaming angry letter from that kid's book about wizards. "I believe this one's for you."

She blinks and looks at my mom, then the plate.

"A brownie?" I ask.

Mom's eyes cut in my direction, and I can feel their sharpness.

"It looks amazing." Sabby's voice is softer than I've ever heard it. "I haven't had one since." She clears her throat. "Thank you."

Mom doles out the rest of the desserts. Kyle jumps right in, *slob*, but Sabby waits. The way her eyes close when she takes the first bite, I'm glad she did, because it meant I got to see it.

She opens her eyes and looks at my mom, tears welling, she says, "It tastes just like my mom made it." She blinks a few times and politely coughs into the crook of her arm. "Thank you."

"Not me, dear. If you know the taste, the kitchen can make it."

Before I can say anything, my girl is up on her feet giving my mom a hug. My heart swells, as does my cock at the little bit of asscheek I can see. My blood boils when I see my brother noticing the same thing. I fling some whipped cream at him, hoping our parents are too wrapped up in the emotion to notice.

"Kris."

Dad's voice rumbles throughout the space.

"Kyle."

Ha, fucker!

Sabby doesn't seem to flinch though. Mom is standing up. She takes her by the hand and they start to leave.

"We're going to have girl time," she says. "The three of you behave."

The door closes behind them, and before Kyle and I can go head to head my dad raises his arms.

"Seems like a game of Monopoly will do you both good. Kris it's your call."

"Whichever one Kyle thinks he's best at."

Dad shakes his head, my brother flipping me as he does.

"You're both too much," he says. There's a laughter to his voice that tells me he wishes he had siblings. "And Kris?"

I look up at him.

"Next time try to wash up before you come home. You smell like a wild beast."

"Definitely smells better on her than you."

Before I can respond Dad's hand is on my shoulder.

"Roll."

I look down at the game board. Typical, I think, seeing the Christmas-themed game board before us.

Kyle rolls a three. I roll a six. Dad comes in with a two. I gather both dice and start the game. Before I know it I'm one train station away from owning all four, not that that's what they're called in this version.

Time moves differently here. I can only imagine what my mom is saying to Sabby. It's probably good for them to chat. Before she met my dad she was a school teacher in Germany, or so they've told me. Each of us has gotten a different version of how they met.

My oldest brother swears her name used to be Gertrude and she was a missionary outside of Philadelphia. He's wrong, but you can't tell him that. Either way, she found love before she found the role of Mrs. Claus.

I think Sabby loves me, or could again. I roll the dice and move seven places, "Score!" The last reindeer is mine! I hear my brother groan and the door open. Out of the corner of my eye I see Sabby, arm in arm with my mom, looking happy as a peach.

Not all hope is lost.

I'm walking on cloud nine. Literally, the slippers Mrs. C—— Jessica—gave me are as comfortable as a cumulus cloud looks. Hence the name Cloud Nine. She asked me when we got in the hall if I was more shocked by the Santa news, or the fact that he—possibly—loves me.

Talking with her was just as warm and gooey as the brownie, which the elves—I mean, again, the fuck, right—were able to whip up a second time. Jessica even wrote it out for me, her script as lovely as she is. I plan on making them for my dad next time I get [...]. We both love them, but before she died, we had my mom.

[...] told me her story, how she met Kris and then saved him [...] rebel, albeit with a cause, behavior. I'd asked her then if [...]Claus is Comin' to Town' was true.

["]Embellished but not completely wrong," had been her response. The magic, the elves, it all seems ridiculous, but next to the fact that Kris probably loves me? I take a breath before we go back into the room I now know is Santa's office.

He's sitting on the floor, on his knees, watching every square his brother moves his game piece.

[...] he shouts, "That's $200 Kyle, pay up—[...] watching them play Monopoly. [...]

"It was that or have them fight," Santa shrugged.

Santa, like the actual man who comes down chimneys and brings toys to kids, is speaking.

His wife was one thing, but this was the actual man. For a moment I thought I might faint. I feel her hand rub my shoulder leading me forward. Kris is still staring at Kyle. My heart swoons, *traitor*. His confession still rings in my mind. I sigh and look over at the game.

"You own all four railroads?"

"They're reindeer in this game," Kris says.

"Doesn't change that he owns them all," Kyle groans.

"Did you not land on one beforehand?"

I ask Kyle.

"No," Kris laughs. "He did, but he had spent all his money on Park Avenue and didn't have the money. I did though."

I walk closer and lean over Kris' shoulder.

"And you have the utilities?" Kris nods. "Hmm."

Moving over to Kyle's side I take inventory of his properties. I notice the first two on the board are up for grabs. I drop my body until my lips are next to Kyle's ear and I whisper, "go for the purples. When you do, build as fast as you can. You have the utilities already. It'll finance your build around the square."

He looks up at me and raises his eyebrow.

He takes my advice. Both of their parents left a little bit ago, leaving an open invite for dinner anytime. When Kyle adds the last hotel he can, he gives me a high-five.

"What the fuck man?"

Kris growls.

"Thank you, Sabby."

"You helped him?"

Kris is looking at me with wide eyes.

"You kidnapped me."

He opened his mouth and closed it again. Kyle roared with laughter.

"You're helping my brother to kick my ass," he says.

"No, I simply pointed out what I would have done if I was him."

"You didn't help me!"

"Did you ask?"

"Did he?"

"You're just pissed because you're losing," Kyle chimes in.

"You're both in deep shit for this," he says.

I give him a look, one I know will only egg him on. His dad might be known for giving presents, but I love when my Santa Daddy doles out punishments.

We hang out a little longer, just long enough to confirm that there was no coming back for Kris, before they call it a game. The two brothers shake hands.

Kyle pulls me into a hug.

"It's great to meet you," he says. "Thank you for your help. Hopefully I'll see you soon."

"Definitely."

I smile as he releases me and turn back to Kris.

"Ready traitor?"

"Sure am."

I wink as I let him lead me to a wall. My eyes roam the rows and rows of pictures. It's like a museum.

"Who are all these people?"

"Santas," Kris says.

He's standing next to me. My heart shouldn't be fluttering but it is. There's a mutiny afoot and it's not *me* helping *his brother.*

"You're kidding?"

"Nope, all the way back to the first one."

He lifts a finger to the top left corner of the wall. I would need binoculars to see it clearly.

"Another day you'll have to explain this all to me again."

He's looking at me. His eyes are even more alive here and I can't decipher what he's thinking.

"Okay, Zabaglione."

I scan the pictures I can see. Not a bad looking man in this guy's whole family.

"If you're done ogling my deceased relatives, we can hit the road."

"It's okay to tell him he's not good-looking enough to make it to the wall," Kyle calls from the couch.

"Fuck off," he shouts back. He takes my hand. "Come on."

I close my eyes and let him lead me. We stop and I feel his breath on my ear.

"You can keep them open," he says.

"But you made me close them on the way in," I say.

"To set the mood!" I lift my brow, feeling my dimple pop as I smirk. "Then again," before I can protest I feel his fingers cover my eyes. "Having you blindfolded is exciting."

I can feel his cock, solid and hard, pressing into me. I rest my body backwards into him.

"Don't start until you've left the room."

Kyle's voice sounds equal parts annoyed and amused. It'd be different if I was *his* sister, but I'm not. Boys are so weird.

Kris pulls me further into him and I hear a door opening. He lifts me off the ground and starts to walk. I can't see, but anything but the air tastes and feels different. It sounds like we're in the woods, far from the insulated and fuzzy world of his dad's office.

"Are you ready for your punishment, my little dessert?"

His hands leave my face and I blink. We're back in the cabin, standing like we just walked in the back door.

"My sweet Sabby soured playing against me."

His words are ridiculous, but his voice, which sounds like he swallowed gravel, is heavy with want. It's enough to make me weak in the knees.

I go to nod on instinct, but I want to know how far he'll push. So instead, I shake my head.

"No," I say.

Kris' grip on my arms tightens. I can feel the charge coming off him. I'm about to get my ass handed to me. My arousal drips down my leg.

"So you don't think you should be punished for making me lose?"

I shake my head again.

"What about pleasuring yourself to other men?"

"You already punished me for that," I say.

His cock twitches against me.

"Obviously not enough," he growls.

His fingers trail down my arms digging into my muscle. The tips leave my skin and I take off further into the cabin. The sports bra isn't enough to keep my bobs from still bouncing. The movement is painful in a weirdly pleasurable way.

It didn't help that I could hear Kris make some kind of animalistic noise as I took off. He sounded like if he caught me he would rip me to shreds. I squealed at the prospect.

"Run as far as you like, Sabby." The front door opens a crack. "When I catch you, I'm going to destroy you."

I pull the door the rest of the way and run into the night.

CHAPTER 10
Kris

I watch as the night eats her up. My cock strains against my pajama bottoms. If I wasn't so excited at the thought of chasing her down I'd laugh at the poor gingerbread man being impaled.

I stroll into the woods. The magic that kept her indoors before extends around the parameter so I know she's safe. Just like she can't get out, no one else can get in to take her. I'm the scariest thing she'll find in these woods. The gingerbread man dances as my hard-on twitches.

Sabby's gotten a head start, but she's so chaotic that she doesn't realize she's left a perfect trail through the debris to find her. I'm in no rush, let her panic a little longer.

As I walk into the woods I think about her meeting my parents and Kyle. It wasn't supposed to happen like that, but I'm sure Kyle interfered. He's good at that. Apparently so is Sabby. I can't believe her strategy worked. Next time I'll play against her and see what she's got.

I'm visualizing a game of strip Monopoly when I see that the trail she left stops in front of a large tree. Either she realized she was making it easy or––my eyes roam to the top of the tree.

The edges of her hair whip in the summer breeze giving away

her hiding spot behind the trunk. She didn't climb high enough that she can't jump down when she figures out that I found her. I think about my options, all the while ignoring the ache I have for her.

Perhaps it's cheating, but I throw my voice out into the forest making her think I've moved along. Then I wait until she jumps down. Her knees buckle and she falls onto the ground. I'm glad I sprinkled more elf dust onto her chest before we walked back into the cabin. That would have hurt her more than it would have gotten her off.

"Silly girl," I tell her, standing over her.

She seems equal parts excited and terrified. I love it. She starts scrambling back on her elbows, never once taking her eyes off mine.

I wrap my hand around her neck applying pressure to both sides.

"Remember, red," I whisper in her ear.

I feel her neck flex as she tries to nod. I snake my other hand around her back and under her armpit dragging her up to her feet. I don't want to accidentally cause her some kind of traumatic brain injury from pulling too hard.

Her eyes sparkle as her feet drag across the ground. Something between a grunt and a moan escapes her as I push her against a tree. Still squeezing the sides of her neck, I see her arm begin to lift. I loosen my hold, sliding my free hand down her chest, her side, until I'm between her legs.

She's so wet already. With no warning I plunge my finger inside her, tightening my fingers around her neck. Her body works against my finger bringing her close to the edge.

"Not yet, Sabby." I slip a second finger inside of her. "You don't get to come until I say so. Do you understand me?"

Her body stills. The whites of her eyes are small triangles. My good girl is enjoying being naughty. I play with her, pushing her toward the edge, waiting until she clenches my fingers and then I change my pace. Move my fingers in a different direction throwing her out of rhythm. Each time she groans and grunts.

My cock might split the fabric trying to hold it in. Her bottoms are drenched. The wet cotton cold against my hand. Everything about this Christmas angel drives me insane.

I loosen my grip on her neck again as I remove the three fingers I had in her and replace it with just the one.

"Please, please."

Her cries are like carols to my ears. This time it's the future Mrs. Claus that will be coming all down my fingers, all over my shaft. I want to feel her juices drip down my balls and into my ass. I want all of her--her scent, her come--absorbed into my skin.

I release her throat and tell her to stay. She squeaks, pushing herself further against the tree. I love this girl. She's perfect, and even if it's a punishment, something I forgot bringing her back and forth to the edge, it doesn't mean she can't get off.

I lift her legs around my waist. I can feel as she locks her feet behind me and with a nod I'm not sure she can see in the darkness, I pump two fingers from each hand in and out of her. The right ones slide out as the left ones slide in, each working different sides of her clit.

She gasps for air, each time sounding more like a moan until I feel it. The rush of warmth gushing out, dripping all over me. She giggles after she comes, shivering as my fingers still pass in and out of her.

She's silly to think this will be the end. Her punishment will be hours of pleasure until she has to beg me to stop.

Tabby

Kris withdraws his fingers and I shudder. I have no idea what that man just did to me, but it felt like he re-wired my insides. I have no objections. He lays me on the ground, my body putty in his hands.

He rests my legs on his shoulders.

"Kris?"

I can't see his face, but I can see his teeth glowing in the limited moonlight.

My pussy is still throbbing, coming down from the orgasm he gave me. I buck as his tongue swipes up my center. This fucker is going to kill me with sex.

He sucks on my clit, flicking it with his tongue before fucking the organ inside me. There's no reprieve. His finger finds the sensitive bud as he keeps fucking me with his tongue. Teasing, licking, sucking, nibbling—I feel myself let go when he replaces his teeth with his tongue. Dirt and leaves collect under my nails as I claw at the ground.

He keeps bringing me closer to oblivion and pulling me back down. Each time I feel more desperate, more alive with need. Kris entices me, his one finger nudging my ass while his thumb my clit and his other fingers are pumping me. I can't see what position he's in; my legs are no longer on his shoulders.

"Come for me, Sabby. Right now baby."

I fall apart.

"Such a good slut you are for me."

"Yes," I moan.

Still dripping, I scream when he jams his cock inside of me.

"Do you still have––"

The words get lost.

"One finger inside of you?"

I try to nod, but the earth has shattered and is swallowing me whole. It's too much at the same time that it's everything.

"Because you take me like you were made for me, Sabby."

He says my name and shivers go through me forcing my back to arch. I can feel myself getting closer and closer all over again.

"You're my good girl, aren't you?"

I nod. My body bucking against his.

SMACK

There's a sting across my face and replaced suddenly with pressure building. I can feel his hand wrapped around my neck.

"My good, Zabaglione. I'm going to choke you until I come."

My eyes roll back into my head. He removes his finger continuing to thrust into me. With his free arm he angles me so my ass is off the ground; he's so deep, I swear he's rearranging the organs in my stomach.

The pressure is building. The sounds of his grunts, his skin slapping against mine is fading behind a ringing, right as the world fades away he howls, releasing my neck.

I gasp for air, crying out through my own orgasm. My walls tighten around him, squeezing him for dear life. I've never come so hard. Ever.

He drops onto the ground next to me, pulling me until I'm cradled alongside him. I shiver and yawn. He smells like the woods, like happiness.

I'm drifting off to sleep when I hear his voice, low and throaty.

"Good night, Sabby."

My answer comes out in a "MmMm." Gingerbread men are dancing in cotton candy clouds and in the distance it sounds like a rumble of thunder is saying "I love you."

* * *

I look up at the bursts of lights coming through the trees. The air feels like it's going to be a hot one once the sun has worked its way into the sky. Kris' arm is wrapped around my shoulders keeping me tucked into him, his legs have woven themselves into mine; it's like he's made some sort of protective cage for me.

If anyone had been watching us the past 24-hours they would think it would be him I need protecting from. Chills run down my body, despite the temperature, thinking of the things that man does to me. I shift and his grip tightens around me, pulling us somehow closer together.

"Good morning."

His voice sounds like someone hooked it up to a trailer and dragged it for miles.

"Morning," I say.

The muscles of his chest absorb my response. He bends his head down and kisses the top of mine. I look down his body. The dips of his muscles, his cock standing straight like a sundial.

"That time already?"

"It's always that time whenever you're around."

I roll my eyes knowing he can't see them.

He rolls me on top of him, but before my body presses down on his, I arch my back careful to keep my nipples off his chest.

"Oof," he says. "Forgot about those."

"You forgot!" I shriek. "You're the one that shoved a needle through them last night."

He lifts his head off the ground and I follow his eyes.

"Are you examining your work?"

He bites his knuckle.

"Actually your tits, but the handiwork isn't bad either."

I look down. Without having a mirror to study them in, it does look like he did a good job from here.

"I actually thought it would hurt more."

He tucks his hands behind his head and rests his head on them.

"About that," he says. I shift my body further down so he's resting against my ass. "I might have helped."

"Helped with what?"

"The pain thing." I blink, watching his face, waiting for some kind of response. "Would you believe me if I told you I had help from some special elf dust?"

Laughter erupts from me shaking both of our bodies. I throw my head back unable to control myself.

"You used elf dust?"

He smiles and nods.

"To pierce my nipples?"

We're both in hysterics now. Not even the grip of his hands on my hips to steady me brings me down.

It's ridiculous––he is ridiculous––and endearing.

"I wanted to make sure it didn't hurt too bad, or worse, get infected."

I lean forward, tucking my head between his neck and shoulder unsure of what to say.

My heart wants to swoon, but my head keeps reminding me of what happened last time I let this man stuff my stocking. I groan a little.

"What? Are you okay?"

"I've been spending too much time with you."

"Why?"

"I made some kind of present pun."

His eyes light up.

"Really?"

"I'm chalking it up to fatigue."

"Tell me," he says.

"No."

His grip tightens on my thighs forcing a different sound from my lips.

"I was thinking about what happened the last time I let you stuff my stocking," I repeat.

The smile fades and the pressure from his finger lessens.

"I'm sorry, Zabaglione." He sighs. My body rises and falls with his. "We had a family emergency—"

"Not Santa! Or your mom. She's so sweet."

Did I really just ask about fucking-Santa-Claus?

"No, not that kind of emergency."

"It was March. Christmas is in December."

He grunts, sliding his body upright, so I'm straddling his lap. My legs wrap about his back like we've done this a million times. We haven't but I'd be happy to practice nine hundred ninety-nine thousand nine hundred ninety-nine more times to make it so.

"There was an issue between our two oldest, and biggest, elf families."

This time I laugh so hard I snort. When I can open my eyes, the sincerity in his pushes me into nervous laughter. He shakes his head and moves his fingers to my sides. He brushes them lightly against my skin and the sensation nearly makes me pee.

"The debate between manufactured electronics and good old fashioned toys is a real one, I'll have you know."

He stops tickling me and I'm able to breathe again.

"What happens when it's all just gift cards, game boys, and whatever else people buy online?"

"The less people believe the less magic we have. Eventually we'll have just enough to survive up here, but there won't be presents from Santa anymore."

"At all?"

"We'll still create and get them to toy drives, hospitals, and things like that. But as far as people are concerned. We'll be myths."

A sadness runs through my chest. I love that they'll help the less fortunate, but what happens to their purpose? Their family?

"Hey," he says, tucking his fingers under my chin and lifting my head. "It's a long ways off. Don't worry by the time we're running the show the magic of Christmas will have returned."

I tilt my head. He slides his hand up along the side.

"Though, you might be the first pierced Mrs. Claus."

He stops talking. His mouth bobbing like a fish. I notice the pink in his cheeks that isn't from the weather. We're not in the North Pole and already the temps gone up.

"I just mean."

"What?"

I ask him, nuzzling against his hand.

"Just that."

"Mhmm."

"I'm sorry about March. Not as sorry as you'll be for sleeping with a leprechaun."

"Laoise?"

"Can you not say her name while you're straddling me?"

"Was a leprechaun."

"Were you going to ignore the clover tattoo she left you?"

"I don't--"

My arms are flat on the ground from my elbows to my wrists, and Kris has one hand under my hip and the other wrapped in my hair. He pulls back forcing my head and my ass to lift.

"Look," he says.

He steers my head and out of the corner of my eye I can see the green leaf I had forgotten about. Instantly the memories of Laoise, the jet-setting woman I met on my trip to England flashes through my mind.

Well fuck me sideways. I look back over my shoulder, Kris could literally take me like this--

"Wait," I snap. "If you hadn't ghosted me I wouldn't have hooked up with anyone else."

He puts my legs back on the ground and walks in a circle around me.

"That's what I'm trying to apologize for."

"You were trying to tell me no Mrs. Claus has ever had pierced nips."

"It's all the same thing." He stops moving and faces me. "I don't want to disappoint you, I don't want you to think I'm some psycho--" we both glance down at my chest. "--I just want you. I want to be able to talk to you and."

"You have a cell phone, and my number"

"They don't really work up here."

"Seems like an excuse."

"I have a solution, but it required me to tell you the truth first."

"That your dad is Santa and I fucked a leprechaun." I throw my hands up. "Also, aren't leprechauns always male?"

"They're kind of like clownfish and snails. They have to keep the line going so at some point, when it's about time for a new generation some of the community will transition over."

"Why?"

"Leprechauns are supposed to be full of trickery, they're foolish little fuckers. Women would be too smart and the breed would die out. Laoise, as you call her, is a great example. She's been using her skills to create a small business empire. Also, why she spends most of her time anywhere but Ireland. Her clan doesn't want her since she tricked them out of forcing her to breed."

"Damn," I say. "Can I have her number for Christmas?"

Kris glowers at me and I take off running through the woods again. This time back toward the cabin.

"Joke or no joke, Zabaglione. When I catch you, I'm going to fuck you, and then I'm going to keep you. I'll spend the rest of my very long life convincing you to be my wife."

His voice booms around me.

"You're wrong," I call back, running as fast as I can manage.

He doesn't have to convince me to be his wife. He's had me tied up in a popcorn chain since I met him. That doesn't change the fact that no matter how good his candy candy is, or how well he trims my tree and fills me with his Christmas custard, he isn't on some kind of probationary period.

I hear his footsteps behind me. I step inside the cabin, surprised by what I see. Christmas has thrown up everywhere. There's tinsel, stockings, fake snow lining the windows. It's too much to process everything at once.

That's when he grabs me. I shriek as he lifts me into the air. He places me down in front of the thickest tree I've seen in my life.

"I'm going to tie you up, and unwrap you with my teeth," he says.

I shiver already anticipating how the afternoon will go. "Because you're the best present I've ever gotten Sabby, and I mean it when I say I want you as my wife one day."

"You'll have to ask first," I tease.

"You're still mine for the next two weeks, remember?" I roll my eyes. He wraps me in ribbons, up and down my body. I gasp as my body swifts and my face seems to plummet to the floor. "I'm going to have my dessert," he says.

I open my eyes and see the room upside down. It takes a second, but I register the cold metal between my fingers.

"Did you hang me on a hook?"

"Every stocking needs to get hung before it can be stuff, Sabby." He steps in front of me, very naked and very hard. "But before we get to stockings and *my* dessert. I have a candy cane for you to choke on."

My mouth parts. Before I can finish my thought about how lame his puns are he slams his cock to the back of my throat. I gag, tears welling in my eyes.

"That's my good girl," he grunts.

I shudder and realize that no one will love Santa as much as I do.

About the Author

Libby Scores is a lot of things, including a writer of smut. To learn more about her and the rest of the holiday series of naught novellas: https://www.easeverything.com/

Thank you for reading!!!

Want More?

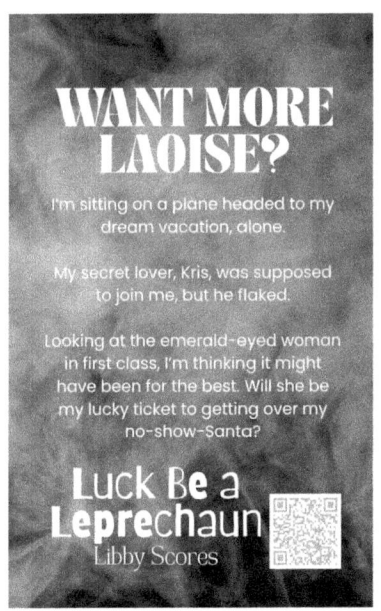